The Mouse
— in the —
Hammock
a Christmas Tale

by BETHANY BREVARD
art by MARCIN PIWOWARSKI

DREAM BIG PUBLISHING, LLC
AUSTIN, TEXAS

It happens this time every year...I hear the attic door going **CREAK** as it slowly opens. The dust on the old, battered box gets wiped away. Its lid is gently lifted, and one by one, we are all taken out.

The tinsel, the ornaments,
the nativity set, the nutcracker,
the angels, and, at last,
little old me.

I peek outside the window with my tiny black eyes. Are those twinkly lights I see? Is that a Christmas tree I smell? Are those jingly bells I hear? This can only mean one thing...

Christmas is near!

No time to dilly-dally. There is so much to do!

The streets are busy with grownups rushing around,

taking care of all the **BIG** things:

the parties, the food, the presents.

But what about the little things? You know, all those things that don't look important but make Christmas extra special. Who will take care of the little things?

Why, someone very little, of course!

So little, he could live in a gingerbread house.

So little, he could sleep in a Christmas tree.

So little, he could hide under a gold bell.

Someone like me,

the Mouse in the

Hammock.

Dong Dong!

As the old clock strikes midnight, my mission begins. I perk up my ears to make sure that no one's awake, I carefully get out of my hammock, climb down the tree branches, and I scurry around the house, looking for all those little things that need doing.

On the first night, I refill the cookie jar...

checking that they still taste good!

Yum!

On the second night, I sew up

the Christmas stocking.

The one with the hole.

ouch!

On the third night, I hang the mistletoe to welcome all who visit our house.

Smooch!

I work so hard each night before Christmas...and I get very sleepy... sometimes so sleepy that I don't make it back to the Christmas Tree.

But I can always count on little hands
to find me and tuck me back into
my hammock so all day long
I can rest up for the night.

ZZZ...ZZZ...

Night after night, my mission continues. I gather the kids' wish lists, I shine the Christmas ornaments, I straighten the star at the top of the tree.

At last
Christmas
Eve arrives!
I just love
Christmas Eve!

Hurray!

All of the friends and family coming to visit!

Patiently I wait for the festivities to end, the

friends to leave and my family to fall fast asleep.

For this is my busiest night of the year.

Santa is on his way and I am his

BIGGEST LITTLE helper.

First, I tiptoe to the manger
where Baby Jesus sleeps
and I gently tuck him in,
for he is little too.

Shhhh!

Then, I make sure that everything is ready for Santa's arrival. Oh no! There's a hot coal in the fireplace! So I quickly pour water on it to put it out.

Splash!

Oh dear! The house is too dark!

So I run to plug in the Christmas tree lights.

Tah-Dah!

Oh my! The cocoa for Santa is too hot!

So I blow on it.

Puff-Puff!

Suddenly, I hear a THUD coming from the chimney.

"Ho, Ho, Ho, Merry Christmas, Little Mouse,"

says Santa, looking around.

"Good work, my dear mouse; getting the house
ready for Christmas is no easy task."

He lifts me up in the palm of his hands and adds,
"This gift is for you, to say thank you for all the
little things that you've done."

Ding-ding,

goes the beautiful gold bell.

"You may think that you've done only little things.
But you don't have to be big to do good things.
The little things make a big difference."

"Now it's getting late and it's time for you to
get some rest," he says, carrying me to my
hammock and tucking me in.

"Merry Christmas, LITTLE Mouse!"

The Mouse in the Hammock,
a Christmas Eve Tale

'Tis the night before Christmas,
And all through the house
Not a creature is stirring
Except one little mouse...

He's just a stuffed toy,
The children believe,
Tucked into his hammock
Which hangs in the tree.

But this Christmas Mouse
Can think and can feel!
He's only pretending to sleep—
He is real!

At midnight he rises,
Makes nary a peep,
Not a sigh nor a murmur,
Not even a squeak.

He jumps from his hammock,
So much to be done.
He blows on the cocoa,
Too hot for the tongue.

He taste-tests the cookies
And straightens the stack.
He starts to take one
But then puts it back.

He climbs to the stockings
Hanging with care.
All except one,
So he makes his repair.

Down from the mantle,
He darts to the spot
Where Santa will land—
And yikes! It's still hot!

Mouse quickly pushes
The embers away.
Saint Nick will be safe
When he leaps from his sleigh.

Now to the manger
Where Jesus, so small,
Inspires our faith,
His love for us all.

Mouse lays a blanket
On our newborn King.
The bells in the morning,
For Him, they will ring.

Oops! The house is too dark
For Santa to see.
Mouse zips to the lights
And plugs in the tree.

But, wait, what's that jingle?
Could Santa be here?
Down the chimney he whooshes,
Lands flat on his rear.

"Good work, little mouse!"
Santa says with a smile.
"Preparing the house
Sure takes quite a while."

"But now it is late,
You best get to bed.
Climb into your hammock
And rest your sweet head."

Tiptoeing to the chimney,
Santa whispers, "Sleep tight!
Merry Christmas, little mouse,
And to all a good night!"

Add the Mouse and the Hammock to Your Christmas Family Traditions!

The Mouse in the Hammock Christmas Tree Ornament is available on Amazon.com and TheMouseInTheHammock.com.

Why a Mouse?

Like many other parents, I felt that my children had started to believe Christmas was about getting presents and me, me, me....

As parents, we want to teach our children to care for others and to learn that even a small gesture of kindness can make a great difference to someone else. After all, isn't Christmas about the joy of giving?

How can we teach a five-year-old to give when they feel so little?

So, at Christmas, a little caring and generous mouse, who sleeps in a hammock, appears on our tree and scurries around the house doing good deeds...

Our Family Story

The original Mouse in the Hammock has been a family heirloom for generations. It's a highly treasured Christmas tree decoration. It has brightened up our Christmas trees for years and I love the idea that it will continue to do so for children all over the world.

**100% Wool
Handmade in Nepal,
Designed in Austin, TX**

**Companion to
*The Mouse in the Hammock,
a Christmas Tale*
children's book**

Mouse and Hammock Christmas Tree Ornament

Size of Mouse: 3" tall; Size of Hammock: 3" wide by 15" long

What are moms saying about *The Mouse in the Hammock, a Christmas Tale* book?

"The Mouse in the Hammock, A Christmas Tale" is a sweet story that helps to bring the focus back to what the true meaning of Christmas really is—Jesus and doing for others! The message that you're never too little to make a big difference is simple, meaningful, and easy for our little ones to apply. And seeing the "pay it forward" and "give back" impacts at the end of the book are so sweet! We love that by purchasing this book we are not only able to teach our children a beautiful message, but also make an impact by helping to provide dignified jobs in Nepal and help provide for the children in the Haitian orphanage. Mouse and his hammock are super cute and we can't wait to hang ours in the tree. And who knows...our little Mouse and his hammock might need to stay out all year round!"
-Amy R. 2019

Little Mouse's Mission

Did you know that small things can make a BIG difference?

We truly believe that!

You might not realize it, but by simply buying this book you have done something BIG.

You have made a BIG difference to all the women who work in our Fair-Trade factory in Nepal. They have lovingly made your mouse and his hammock, in return for fair wages, education and health care for themselves as well as their children.

Pay it forward: Supporting fair trade. Factory in Nepal where Mouse and hammock are handmade by local artisans.

You have made a BIG difference to the children from the Maison des Enfant de Dieu (House of the Children of the Lord), an orphanage in Haiti that is home to over 60 children who have, sadly, lost everything. We believe every child needs a safe place to sleep and education so a portion of the proceeds from your book purchase goes to them.

To learn more about Maison des Enfant de Dieu, please visit www.teemhaiti.com.

Just like the mouse in our story, you may be small, but you can make a BIG difference.

To see all the little things that Mouse is doing to make a BIG difference in the world, follow him on Instagram, #mouseinthehammock.

Pay it back: Every child needs a safe place to sleep and education. Portion of proceeds support Orphanage in Haiti.

To Josh: Thank you for loving me and supporting our crazy dreams.
La Buena Vida

To Riley: I love that you give me your honest opinion,
which I hold in the highest regards.

To Cole: Your creativity and out-of-the-box thinking leads me
to new ideas and different ways of seeing the world.

JBRC: Dream Big!

To my mom and dad for their loving support and
our family's original 1970's Mouse in the Hammock.

Special thank you to Marcin: for bringing our little mouse to life
and illustrating his personality and gentle soul. May our little mouse
bless the lives of all those who meet him.

Thank you to my amazing team: Story Editor, Laura Caputo-Wickham,
Rhyming Editor, Michelle Turner, and Layout Designer, Jodi Giddings.
Without these talented ladies our mouse in the hammock
would still be running around my house instead
of sharing his good deeds with the world.

DREAM BIG PUBLISHING, LLC, AUSTIN, TEXAS

Illustrations by Marcin Piwowarski

ISBN-13: 978-1-7331529-1-4

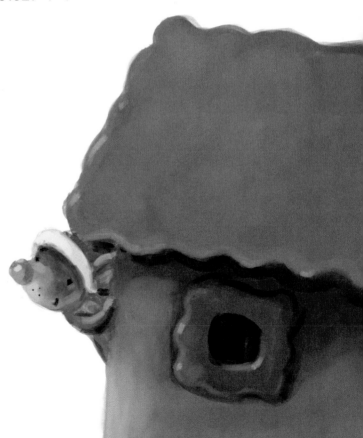

Made in the USA
Monee, IL
25 November 2022